Text copyright © 2003 by Kate Banks
Pictures copyright © 2003 by Tomek Bogacki
All rights reserved
Distributed in Canada by Douglas & McIntyre Ltd.
Color separations by Hong Kong Scanner Arts
Printed and bound in the United States of America by Phoenix Color Corporation
Designed by Nancy Goldenberg
First edition, 2003
10 9 8 7 6 5 4 3 2 1

Library of Congress Cataloging-in-Publication Data
Banks, Kate, 1960–
    Mama's coming home / Kate Banks ; pictures by Tomek Bogacki.
      p. cm.
    Summary: Papa prepares dinner and the boys set the table as they, the dog, and the cat
eagerly await Mama's return home after work.
    ISBN 0-374-34747-6
    [1. Working mothers—Fiction.   2. Sex role—Fiction.   3. Family life—Fiction.]   I. Bogacki,
Tomasz, ill.   II. Title.

PZ7.B22594 Maj 2003
[E]—dc21
                                      2002067922

Mama's Coming Home

KATE BANKS

pictures by TOMEK BOGACKI

FRANCES FOSTER BOOKS · FARRAR, STRAUS AND GIROUX · NEW YORK

The clock goes ticktock on the wall.
The phone is ringing down the hall.

Shops are closing for the day.

Mama's coming home.

Papa turns the oven on.
Ties an apron round his waist.

Horns are blaring. Whistles blowing.
Mama's coming home.

Boys are sprawling on the floor.
Baby's crawling toward the door.

The sidewalk throbs with footsteps.
Mama's coming home.

Papa's rolling pizza dough.
Laying sausage row by row.

The station platform fills with crowds.

Mama's coming home.

The dog is howling loudly.
Growling at the cat.

The train moves slowly down the track.
Mama's coming home.

Papa feeds the baby.
Scolds the boys, the dog, the cat.
"Mama's coming home!" he says.

People clamber off the train.
Clouds are swelling fast with rain.
Mama's coming home.

Now the dog is munching.
Crunching on a bone.

Thunder clapping. Raincoats flapping.

Mama's coming home.

Boys have got the table made.
Laid with plates and silverware.

Eager feet are hastening.
Mama's coming home.

Baby's legs are turning.
Churning like a riverboat.

The streetlights flicker on like stars.
Mama's coming home.

Boys are picking up their toys.
The cat is licking doggy's ears.

Footsteps hurry up the walk.

Mama's coming home.

Little faces beaming.
Gleaming in the windowpane.

Kisses flying. No more crying.

Mama's at the door . . .

Mama's home!